DANGER! ACTION! TROUBLE! ADVENTURE!

THE D.A.T.A SET

Down the Brain Drain

By Ada Hopper
Illustrated by Rafael Kirschner of Glass House Graphics

LITTLE SIMON
New York London Toronto Sydney New Delhi

This book is a work of fiction. Any references to historical events, real people, or real places are used fictiously. Other names, characters, places, and events are products of the author's imagination, and any resemblance to actual events or places or persons, living or dead, is entirely coincidental.

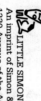
LITTLE SIMON

An imprint of Simon & Schuster Children's Publishing Division
1230 Avenue of the Americas, New York, New York 10020
First Little Simon paperback edition July 2020
Copyright © 2020 by Simon & Schuster, Inc.
Also available in a Little Simon hardcover edition

All rights reserved, including the right of reproduction in whole or in part in any form.
LITTLE SIMON is a registered trademark of Simon & Schuster, Inc., and associated colophon is a trademark of Simon & Schuster, Inc.

For information about special discounts for bulk purchases, please contact Simon & Schuster Special Sales at 1-866-506-1949 or business@simonandschuster.com.
The Simon & Schuster Speakers Bureau can bring authors to your live event. For more information or to book an event contact the Simon & Schuster Speakers Bureau at 1-866-248-3049 or visit our website at www.simonspeakers.com.
Designed by Jay Colvin
Manufactured in the United States of America 0620 BVG
10 9 8 7 6 5 4 3 2 1
This book has been cataloged with the Library of Congress.
ISBN 978-1-5344-1130-2 (hc)
ISBN 978-1-5344-1129-6 (pbk)
ISBN 978-1-5344-1131-9 (eBook)

CONTENTS

Chapter 1

An Icky Little Problem

"Don't look now, but the enzymes are coming! Breaking down food to keep your body running. Proteins, fats, and sugars all do their part. Absorb into your bloodstream and pump that heart!"

Gabe, Laura, and Olive clapped as Cesar did a mic drop. The four science whiz kids, known as the DATA Set, were rehearsing their presentations on the human body in Dr. Bunsen's laboratory.

"What did you guys think of my rap?" Cesar asked.

The three friends whispered quietly like judges on a panel.

"It was a little pitchy," Olive said at last.

Cesar's face dropped. "It was?"

"Yes, as in . . . pitch *perfect*!" Olive cried. "I bet you're the only student who will rap a song for their presentation!"

Cesar pulled out a pair of sunglasses. With them on, he looked like a super cool rock star!

"Oh, you know, just doing my part to keep the DATA Set fresh," Cesar said, giving Olive a high five.

Their classmates at school were probably expecting each DATA Set presentation to be accurate and scientific. But Cesar had just proved that sometimes it was important to spice things up.

Right then, Dr. Bunsen appeared in front of the kids. Normally, he was in his lab when they came to visit, but today there was a bright glow around him as he greeted them as a hologram.

"Hello there, DATA Set friends," the doctor said in a scratchy voice.

"Dr. B., your voice sounds horrible," said Cesar.

"And where are you right now?" Gabe added. "This hologram device is super cool!"

"I'm at a convention," Dr. Bunsen explained. "But I'm not feeling so good right now."

"It sounds like it's just a bad cold," Laura said. "With some rest, you should be fine in a few days!"

"Ah, but I don't have a few days!" the doctor cried. "I need to present my invention at the National Council for Creative Cures in *three* hours.

All the top scientists in the world
will be here soon."

"No way! What are you going to
be talking about?" Olive asked.

"The cure for the common cold,"
he replied as he looked down and
let out a big sigh.

"Wow, what are the chances!" Cesar said with a laugh.

"Oh, this was all part of my plan!" Bunsen declared as his eyes lit up. "And you four are my only hope for getting better in time!"

"Uh, Dr. B., you know we can't *cure* your cold, right?" Gabe asked. "I think that might be your high fever talking."

"Ah, believe it or not, you *can* cure me . . . with the teeny-tiny but mighty device I left under my microscope. Behold, the Bunsen Cold Buster 3000!"

Through the lens, the kids saw a device that looked like a submarine! It had a large window, a big steering wheel, a porthole at the top, and two wings on the side.

"Whoa. Is this a supercharged vitamin C pill?" asked Cesar.

"Oh, it's much better than that.

This microscopic vehicle, which can be swallowed like a pill, can dive into the human body and kick out my cold!" Dr. B cried. "And you four will be the first to drive it."

Chapter 2

Herm the Germ

"You mean we're going to travel inside your body? That's so cool!" Laura exclaimed.

"Um, is 'cool' really the word to use?" Cesar asked. "I can think of a few others. Like dangerous. Untested. Slimy—"

"Sign us up!" Gabe cut in.

"Great! I've programmed the ship so that you guys will fly to where I am. But first, put on the green wet suits on the table. They're made with top secret germ-proof material so you'll be fully protected."

The kids quickly put them on and within minutes everyone was ready to go.

"Okay. You've all got one hour. I'm counting on you!"

"Don't worry, Dr. B.," Cesar said, shaking his hologram hand. "We'll kick that cold out of you!"

"Thanks, Cesar! All you need to do is press the button on the back of your suits!" the doctor exclaimed with glee. So the kids looked at one another, took deep breaths, and pressed their buttons at the same time.

ZAP! ZAP! ZAP, ZAP!

Just like that, the DATA Set shrank down to the size of tiny gnats!

Then they climbed into the Cold Buster 3000.

When the kids were all buckled up, the ship flew out of the lab and took them to the convention center. Then the doctor scooped up the ship, placed it gently on his tongue, and took a big gulp of water.

"Hold on tight, guys!" Gabe called out as their ship swirled all the way down Dr. B.'s throat.

Before they knew it, the spinning slowed as they came to a halt.

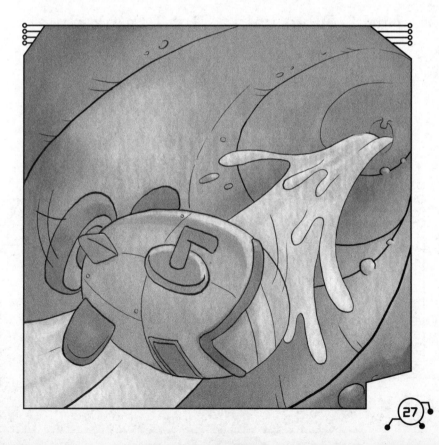

"Umm, that was fast. Are we already inside Dr. B.'s stomach?" Cesar asked. "Because I feel like I might be sick."

"No. Looks like we've hit a dead end," Olive said. "But I think this ship will tell us what to do." The navigation system next to the steering wheel was blinking with a REQUEST HELP sign.

As soon as Olive pressed the screen, Dr. Bunsen's face appeared.

"Welcome aboard! This tiny submarine, designed for travel through the amazing human body, was funded in part by the Council for Creative—"

"Sorry, let's skip the sales pitch, Dr. B.," Gabe said, pushing the fast-forward button.

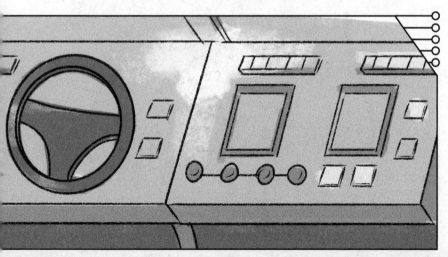

"—your very urgent mission," Dr. Bunsen's voice skipped on, "is to find this slimy creature."

A giant neon-green blob popped up on the screen.

"BUUUURRRLLLGHH!" Cesar gagged. "What is *that*?!"

"I present to you the common cold," Dr. Bunsen continued. "The patented Bug-Catcher nets in your suit pockets will help you capture this creature. You *must* find it before it multiplies too many times. Good luck, my DATA Set friends! My body is counting on you!"

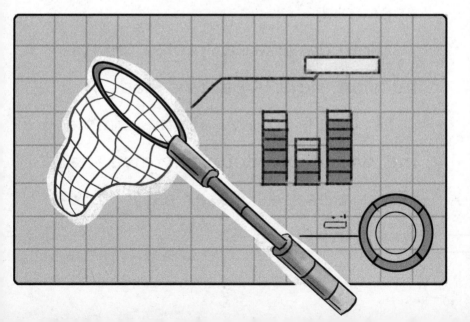

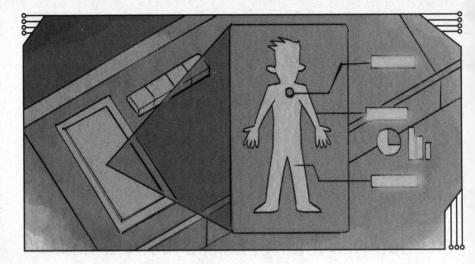

Then Dr. Bunsen's face went away and a map of his body appeared.

"Sounds like a pretty simple mission, right?" Laura asked.

"I don't know about simple, but we should definitely give that thing a name," Cesar said. "Like Herm the Germ—"

BEEP! BEEP! BEEP! BEEP!

An alarm blared out of the speakers as the ship lurched forward and landed in yellow goo!

"Oh man. I think we're stuck in Dr. Bunsen's mucus," Laura said, looking out the window. "His immune system must be using  this goo to fight the virus. Which means—"

"It's right here!" exclaimed Olive. "Look!"

Olive pointed to the glowing creature right in front of them. It was getting closer and closer to the ship.

"Ahhh! It's Herm the Germ!"
Cesar gasped.

That's when Gabe turned around
to announce their game plan.

"Olive, you stay here in case we
need your help," he said. "And,
Laura and Cesar, come on! We've
got to grab it before it gets away!"

Olive opened the door, and Gabe took the lead. The three friends carefully inched closer and closer, until Gabe's net was above the blob. Then, on his signal, they swung their rods as hard as they could.

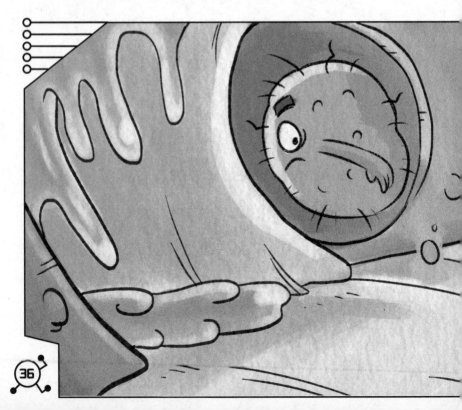

But they were way too slow. The virus latched on to a blood cell, split into three, and zoomed away in opposite directions.

"We have to chase it!" shouted Gabe. "Or we lose it for good!"

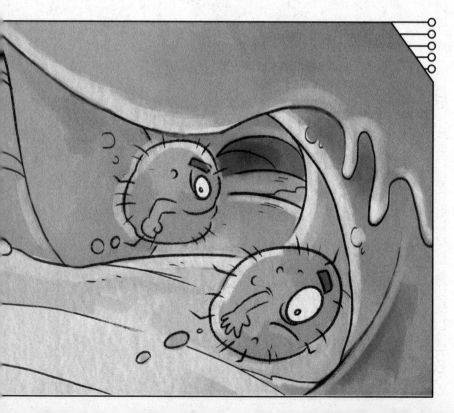

Chapter 3

A Case of Indigestion

Gabe darted right, Laura went left, and Cesar shot straight down, down, down, until . . .

SPLOOSH!

Cesar plunged into an ocean of choppy waters. Floating all around him were bits and pieces of half-digested food.

"Oh my gosh." Cesar gasped as he looked around. "I'm in Dr. B.'s stomach!"

Cesar marveled in amazement as large tortilla chips, a tuna-salad sandwich, and chewed-up pieces of carrots and broccoli passed him.

They were all swimming together
in a brownish-pink soup.

"I love to eat and all, but that is
gross," Cesar said as he watched
a large sardine head
float by.

Then he took
a deep breath and
swam toward the wall
of the stomach. When he reached
the edge, he pulled himself out.

"Thank goodness!" Cesar said
with a sigh. "I can finally bre—"

BEEP! BEEP! BEEP! BEEP!

Cesar looked up in a panic.

"Herm the Germ is back!" he shouted.

A piece of the cold virus attached to the lining of Dr. B.'s stomach. Cesar knew  he needed to follow it, so he flicked open his net and jumped into the wild waves.

"Don't you move one inch," Cesar muttered under his breath. "Don't . . . wiggle . . . another . . ." But as he got closer, the blob moved faster.

"Oh, no you don't!" he cried. Cesar swung his net down, but Herm the Germ was too fast for him! Within seconds, 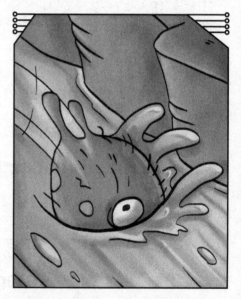 the sneaky virus dropped down into the water and disappeared!

"Pita crumbs!" Cesar yelled out.
"I almost had it."

Right then, the waters began sloshing back and forth violently. Cesar tried his hardest to swim against the current. But it was no use. He was being swept away . . . straight toward the opening of the small intestine!

"Oh no! Cesar cried. He swam in the opposite direction with all his might. "I'm going to get digested!"

"No, you won't!" cried a familiar voice. "Hey, Cesar! Are you there?"

Cesar broke into a big smile as soon as he heard his friend.

"Olive!" Cesar cried. "HELP!"

"I'm coming as fast as I can!" Olive shouted. "Hang on!"

Cesar struggled to keep his head above the water. He could feel his feet getting closer to the opening of the intestinal tube. Flailing his arms, Cesar reached wildly for anything to grab on to until . . . a strong hand clasped his wrist.

"Gotcha!" Olive cried.

Using her net, she pulled her friend to safety and led him back into the submarine. Cesar looked around in awe as four retractable arms extended from the base of the vehicle and latched onto the stomach wall.

"Thanks, Olive!" Cesar cried. "Without you, I would have been swallowed like a pack of sardines!"

"Yeah, that would *not* have been fun," Olive replied. "I'm so glad I found—"

BEEP! BEEP! BEEP! BEEP!

The alarm cut in and Gabe's surprised face popped up on the large screen.

"Gabe needs help. We need to go!" Olive cried.

"Hold on, Cesar. This ride is going to get bumpy!"

Then she pressed down on the gas, and they zoomed out of Bunsen's stomach and up toward the heart.

Chapter 4

Feel the Beat

"Is this how you found me?" Cesar asked in amazement. A group of red blood cells led the way as they sped down a vein tunnel.

Olive nodded. "You bet! When the three of you split up, this map told me where you were right away."

"Oh, thank goodness," Cesar said. "If you hadn't come to get me, I would have gone down Dr. B.'s intestines and come out as . . ." He couldn't bring himself to say it.

"Poop?" Olive asked, finishing his sentence for him.

Cesar shuddered. "Yup. I owe you one."

Olive smiled wide, still focused on the road ahead. Soon Cesar saw on the map that they were getting closer to Bunsen's heart.

THUMP! THUMP! THUMP! THUMP!

They were so close that they could feel the vibrations of the heart shake the ship.

"It feels like there's a disco party going on!" Cesar exclaimed as he bopped to the beat.

When they got to Gabe's location, their eyes grew wide. Dr. B.'s heart looked like a beatbox, shooting brightly colored pulses of blood up through the main arteries.

"Look! There he is!" Cesar cried. Poor Gabe was flopping up and down on Dr. B.'s heart, unable to keep his balance. He was being tossed back and forth like a rag doll in a bouncy house!

"Hang on a second!" Olive yelled through the microphone. "We're  coming for you!"

Olive drove the car forward, but  every time they would get near, another pulse of blood would send Gabe flying out of reach.

"Hey, I have an idea!" shouted Cesar. "Open the door!"

Then he climbed out and stood right under Gabe's body, jumping along to the beat.

"Ready . . . ," Cesar whispered, counting the beats. "Steady . . ."

Cesar focused hard to time his jumps to the rhythm. Then he lifted his arms out in front of him.

"GOTCHA!"

"Whoa!" Gabe cried. "Thanks, Cesar!"

"No problem!" Cesar replied as he helped his friend stand up. Then he led the way to the ship.

"Gabe! Are you okay?" Olive asked worriedly as they came aboard.

"Yeah, I think so," Gabe replied with a smile.

"But I felt like my brain was being scrambled!"

"Did you find Herm the Germ?" Cesar asked eagerly.

"Yes, but only for a split second. Herm was just too fast!" Gabe explained. "And now we have a big problem."

Gabe's face grew serious as he pointed at the neon-green blood pulses that were pumping in the veins of Dr. B.'s arteries.

Hundreds of cold virus cells were now attached to Bunsen's heart. The virus was spreading fast, and the kids were running out of time!

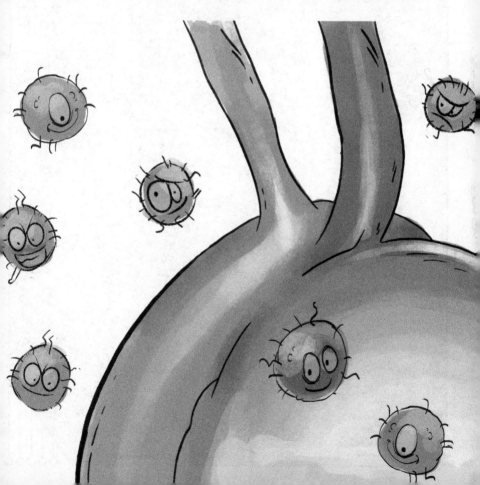

Chapter 5

Authorized Personnel Only

"What are we going to do?" asked Cesar in a panic. "Even with these nets, we can't catch *all* of these germs."

"And we're running out of time!" Gabe yelled. "What was Dr. B. thinking when he was testing this bacteria?"

"Oh, Gabe, that's it! Since we're inside Bunsen's body, we can find out!" Olive cried excitedly. Then she pointed to a blinking light. "Laura is up in Dr. B.'s brain. Maybe she's found a clue!"

It sounded crazy, but it was the best plan they had. So the kids

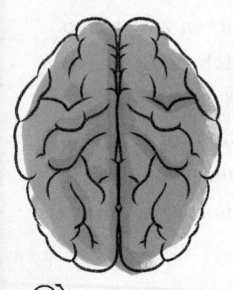

zoomed up along Dr. B.'s spinal cord and all the way up to his brain.

"Whoa!" Gabe yelled when they finally stopped.

"Bunsen's brain looks like a giant maze!"

Stretched out before them were large coils of brain tissue, weaving and winding around one another like long, squishy hallways. Rows of doors lined the sides with shiny silver neurons guarding each one.

"Ever wonder what the inside of a genius mad scientist looks like?" Cesar joked.

"Yeah, and it's even cooler than I imagined!" Gabe cried. "We're actually going to *see* how Dr. B. thinks!"

Olive carefully steered the ship deeper into the center of Dr. B.'s brain until they reached a large door marked MEMORY CONTROL CENTER. AUTHORIZED PERSONNEL ONLY.

The navigation system that was leading them was showing that Laura was inside.

So Olive used the retractable arms she had used in Bunsen's stomach to park the vehicle. And then Gabe slowly opened the window.

They immediately had to shield their eyes. A blinding white light blocked their view. When their vision adjusted, they saw that they were standing in a circular room, surrounded by many screens playing videos of Dr. Bunsen's memories.

"Oh, guys! You found me!" Laura yelled, rushing in for a group hug.

"Laura!" the friends exclaimed. "You're here!"

"Yeah. Dr. Bunsen's brain is amazing," she replied. "I've been watching his life play in front of my eyes!"

The three friends looked around in awe.

"Wow, look over here! There's baby Bunsen!" Cesar cried, pointing to a screen showing an infant giggling up at a mobile made of atoms and molecules. "That was his first pair of goggles!"

"And here he is winning the Inventor of the Year Award," Olive said. "But who's that grumpy guy next to him?"

"That's a doctor he worked with," Gabe said, looking at a second screen. "Clearly, they *used* to be good friends."

Whatever happened during that award ceremony, Dr. Bunsen didn't remember it as a good day.

Right then, Cesar yelled out. "Hey! Here we are!"

A big screen showed clips of the adventures the DATA Set and Dr. B. shared. One screen had their very first meeting when the kids sold him candy bars, while a second one showed the time they helped an alien get back home.

"Why are our screens larger than the other ones?" Cesar asked.

"I think the memories that have meant the most to Dr. B. have the largest screens," Laura explained.

"And believe it or not, one of them has the answer to curing his nasty cold!"

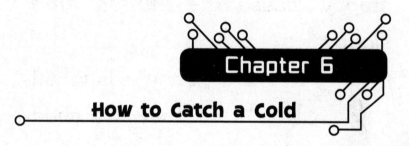

Chapter 6

How to Catch a Cold

Laura brought her friends to the biggest screen, which showed the doctor working in his lab.

"This is Dr. B. making the cold virus," she explained. "He must have been working on it nonstop because it's taking up a lot of his brainpower right now."

"I said a drip, droppy. A Petri to the boppy, and this virus won't stoppy 'cause the Bunsen ain't sloppy."

They laughed as they watched Bunsen beatbox on the screen.

"Hey, what do you know!" Cesar said as he broke into a grin. "Dr. B. can rap too!"

Right then, Dr. Bunsen did an unsteady spin and hit the counter, knocking over his Petri dish! Neon-green goop splattered all over his face.

"So *that's* how Dr. B. got sick," Gabe said as he paused the video. "But how do we kick Herm out?"

"The answer's in the writing!" Laura explained. She pointed to the board behind Dr. Bunsen. The DNA for Herm the Germ was written there in dry-erase marker.

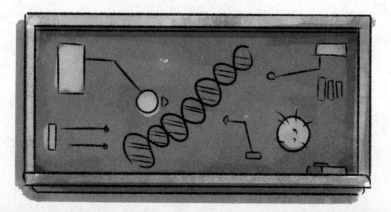

"There are too many copies of Herm now," Laura continued. "But what if we use the submarine's tracking system to make all the Herms come to *us*?"

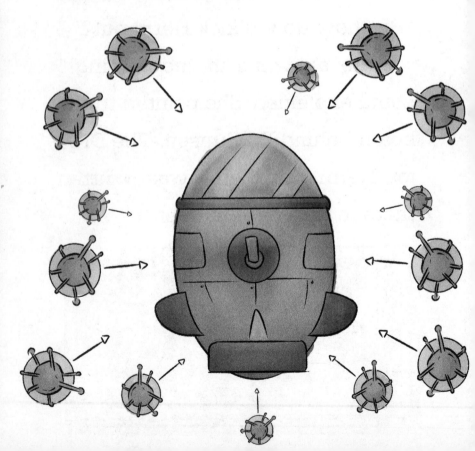

"And make it look like we're the most tasty cells of all?" Cesar asked.

"Exactly," Laura said. Cesar was nervous about letting Herm come close, but it was worth a shot. So Laura and Olive reprogrammed the navigation device using the tools in the glove box that Dr. Bunsen had provided.

Gabe attached his net to the ship's robot arms. The net had a special function that let it expand wide enough to catch all the Herm copies at once.

Meanwhile, Cesar coded the virus's DNA into the ship's computer.

After the final adjustments, everything for Operation Herm the Germ was ready to go.

"We have ten minutes left," Laura said, checking the clock. "Let's go catch Herm once and for all!"

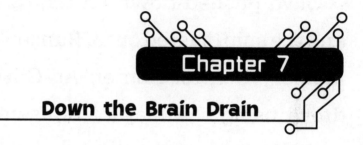

Chapter 7

Down the Brain Drain

One by one, little blinking lights showed up on the ship's screen. Ten. Twenty. A hundred. The screen was covered in lights and the virus cells were getting closer.

"This is crazy!" Cesar yelled as he took a big breath. "Are we sure this is going to work?"

"We're about to find out!" cried Olive. "Hang on!"

Olive pushed down on the gas, and the ship blasted out of Bunsen's Memory Control Center. As Olive drove using the map of Bunsen's body, Laura kept a close eye on the tracking screen.

"We have to make sure the virus keeps chasing us until all

the copies are in range!" she
shouted.

Olive drove through a room that
looked like an upside-down version
of Bunsen's lab. Wacky contraptions
were scattered everywhere.

"These must be where all of Dr. B.'s half-baked ideas live!" Gabe called out with a sparkle in his eye.

They soared through the room, marveling at what they saw, until

they got to another door. In this room, a hologram of Dr. Bunsen performed a dramatic play while holding a plastic skull.

"To Dr. B.? Or not to Dr. B.?" Bunsen proclaimed to an audience of applauding sloths.

"Wow, there are levels to this guy that we don't even *know* about," Cesar said with a laugh. His friends agreed, smiling.

Soon Olive zoomed down a bright-red corridor.

"It's working. We've almost got

them all!" cried Laura, looking through the rearview mirror. "Just a few more to—WHOA!"

The sub suddenly came to a screeching halt.

"Sorry!" Olive apologized. "But look where we are!"

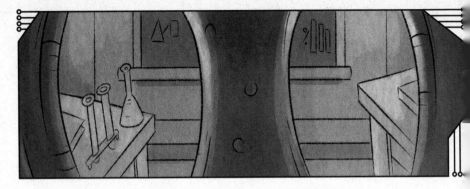

Everyone gasped. They were out of the crazy brain maze and were now sitting behind Bunsen's eyes—actually *seeing* what he was seeing!

"Look! It's his lab!" cried Laura.

"And that clock on the wall says we only have five minutes left!" Gabe yelled out.

"Perfect—that's all the time we need," Laura said confidently.

"Gabe, it's time to activate the net!"

Gabe nodded. But right as his finger was about to press the button, the ship lurched forward. The largest piece of the cold virus smacked into the ship . . . and took the net with it!

The kids held on to their seats as the vehicle shook back and forth.

"NOOOO! Without the net, we'll never catch Herm!" exclaimed Gabe.

"Not only that." Cesar gulped. "But I think the cold has caught *us* instead."

The DATA Set looked around, and Cesar was right. They were totally surrounded!

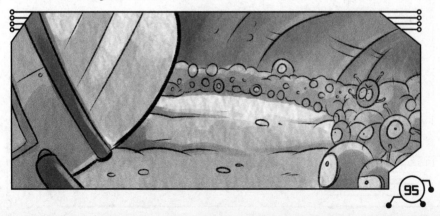

Chapter 8

Getting Boogy

"Hey, Cesar, can you attach your net to the mechanical arms?" Olive asked.

Cesar looked out the porthole. "I don't think so," he replied. "The arms have been damaged, so I don't think they can hold the net anymore."

"Guys, I hate to say it," Laura began. She nervously eyed the thousands of cells closing in around them. "But we may need to lead the cells down to Dr. B.'s bladder and hope his body releases us, too."

"That's not only way too gross, but Dr. B. will also miss his conference!" Olive cried.

"Yeah, he's counting on us!" Gabe agreed. "There's *got* to be a quicker way—after all, we're the *DATA Set*, right?"

"But we're surrounded!" Laura exclaimed.

"You're right," Cesar replied. He looked out at the virus cells, then up at the inside of Dr. Bunsen's head.

"They may be surrounding us. But *we've* got the germ right where we need it!"

"Uhhh, what do you mean?" Gabe asked, confused.

"Now that we've got Herm the Germ and all his crazy cousins in one spot, we can make Bunsen kick the cold out himself!" Cesar continued, growing more excited by the second.

"But his immune system will take days to defeat the virus." Laura shook her head. "And we only have five minutes!"

"Oh, I'm not talking about his immune system," Cesar replied. "I'm talking about a good old sneeze! If we stretch our nets inside Dr. B.'s nose and make him sneeze, the virus will get caught with one big blow!"

Gabe, Laura, and Olive looked at the tracking screen. Their current location had a direct pathway to doctor's nose.

"You're a genius!" Gabe cried. "Come on, it's now or never!"

So Olive turned the ship, pressed down on the pedal, and blasted

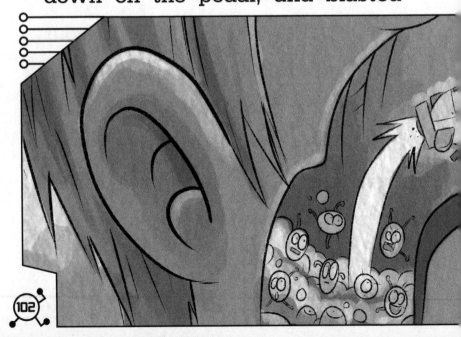

toward Dr. B.'s nose, clearing all the germs that were in front of them. All the other virus cells immediately followed behind, quickly piling into Dr. B.'s nose, just as they'd hoped. Within seconds every copy of Herm was stuck in slimy yellow mucus.

"Yes, they're trapped!" cheered Laura. "Quick! Let's stretch out our nets!"

The DATA Set then climbed out and secured their nets along the wall of Dr. B.'s nose.

"Okay, now we just need to make Dr. B. sneeze," said Cesar. "For that we'll need to get *swinging*!"

Taking Cesar's lead, the friends all jumped up and grabbed onto one of Dr. Bunsen's nose hairs.

"I'm flying!" Cesar yelled as he swung back and forth.

"Hey, look at me! I'm a nasal gymnast!" cried Olive, swinging from one nose hair to the next.

It was the slimiest thing they had ever done in their lives.

And yet . . . it was a lot of fun. In a crazy, boogery sort of way.

"Hey! It's working!" Gabe cried as a rush of wind pushed him to the right. "Quick! Everyone back in the ship!"

The friends scrambled back inside, just as a loud rumbling began.

Chapter 9

The Big Presentation

With a big sneeze, the ship came flying straight out of Dr. B.'s nose! And the cells burst out behind them, tangled inside the net.

The Cold Buster 3000 headed back toward the lab, while Bunsen caught and safely handled the tight, goopy bundle of cells.

As soon as the kids arrived back at Bunsen's, they all hopped out of the vehicle.

Now that they were safely on the ground, it was time to grow big. Just like before, they looked at each other, took deep breaths, and pressed the buttons on their suits.

And just like that, they were back to normal!

"Oh, DATA Set, you did it! I feel so much better. Huzzah! I've been cured!" the doctor exclaimed as his hologram jumped up and down.

"I have safely secured the cells inside a Petri dish, and thanks to you all, I will be in tip-top shape for my presentation," Dr. B. said.

The kids gave Dr. B. a big thumbs up. As always, when they worked together, the doctor and the kids were the perfect team.

It was almost time for Bunsen to get onstage, so they said goodbye, but before going home, they changed and threw their suits away.

Meanwhile, Dr. Bunsen made some final notes for his speech.

Later that evening, the four friends watched Dr. B. on TV.

"The Bunsen Cold Buster 3000 is brand-new," Dr. B. said as he looked directly at the front camera.

"It helps your immune system kick out a cold in half the time!"

"How impressive!" shouted a man with dark-rimmed glasses.

"How did you come up with it?" asked a woman in a sleek business suit.

The doctor smiled. "Oh, I had help from the best research team a scientist could ask for—the DATA Set!" he cried. "Thanks to their research, I've made some final tweaks and my Cold Buster technology will be ready for the masses!"

The doctor then switched on a commercial with him rapping about the benefits of his newest invention.

"Woo-hoo! Hooray for team Buns—*AHHHH-CHOOO!*" Cesar sneezed as he covered his mouth.

"Oh no," he mumbled as his friends safely moved out of the way. "That Herm is one sneaky germ."

Chapter 10

A Team to Count On

The next day the DATA Set presented their school report in their pajamas. A four-way split screen connected them with their class.

"And that's how the left side of the heart pumps oxygen-rich blood up through—*AH-CHOO!*—the arteries—"

PFFFFFFFT! Gabe grabbed a tissue and blew his nose as he covered his face.

"Thank you for presenting your report via video conference so that the rest of the class doesn't get sick," Mrs. Bell said.

"No worries, Mrs. Bell," Laura sad. "Sorry we can't be there in person."

Mrs. Bell nodded her head.

"You four have certainly gone above and beyond for your projects, but please get some rest now."

"We will, Mrs. Bell," the DATA Set promised.

Dr. Bunsen then switched off the screen. He had been running their presentations for them from his lab. "Are you sure you don't want to use the Bunsen Cold Buster

3000?" he asked. "You'd feel better in half the time!"

"Thanks, Dr. B." Olive said. "But right now, I just want some chicken noodle soup."

"Mmmmm. Chicken noodle soup," Cesar said as he rubbed his stomach. Despite his fever, his appetite was still strong.

"Okay. As you please, my DATA Set friends," Dr. Bunsen said. "But I need my research partners back in tip-top shape ASAP!"

Laura nodded. "You got it, Dr. B."

"Yeah, for sure. But this time we'll take care of Herm the Germ the old-fashioned way. With lots of water, sleep, and *no* human body travel," Cesar added.

The DATA Set and Dr. Bunsen all laughed and promised to stay home and get rest until Herm the Germ was out of commission for good.

THE DATA SET

FOR MORE DANGER! ACTION! TROUBLE! ADVENTURE!

Check out all the previous books!